Pip and Posy

www.worldofpipandposy.com

First published 2018 by Nosy Crow Ltd
The Crow's Nest, 14 Baden Place,
Crosby Row, London, SE1 1YW
www.nosycrow.com

This edition first published 2019

ISBN 978 1 78800 541 8

Nosy Crow and associated logos are trademarks and/or registered
trademarks of Nosy Crow Ltd
Text © Nosy Crow Ltd 2018
Illustrations © Axel Scheffler 2018

The right of Axel Scheffler to be identified as the illustrator
of this work has been asserted.

A CIP catalogue record for this book is available from the British Library.

Printed in China
Papers used by Nosy Crow are made from wood grown in sustainable forests.

3 5 7 9 8 6 4

Pip and Posy

The Christmas Tree

Axel Scheffler

nosy crow

It was Christmas time and Pip and Posy
went to fetch a Christmas tree.

When they got home,
they put the tree in a pot.

Then they baked biscuits to hang on it.

The five biscuits looked really pretty.

Posy went to get four candy canes.

But when she came back,
one of the biscuits was missing.

"That's odd," she said. "There were five
biscuits, but now there are only four."

Posy went to find the chocolate bells
while Pip put the candy canes on the tree.

But when Posy came back she noticed that one of the candy canes was missing.

"There were four candy canes," she said. "But now there are only three."

Posy went to get the Christmas star.

Pip put the chocolate bells on the tree.

But when Posy came back she saw that all the decorations had **completely disappeared!**

Oh dear!

Then Posy noticed that Pip was lying on the sofa.

"Are you ok, Pip?" said Posy.

"No," said Pip.

"I feel sick."

Poor Pip!

Posy brought Pip
a glass of water.

"I'm sorry, Posy,"
said Pip.
"I ate ALL the
decorations."

"Yes, I know,"
said Posy.

They decided to go outside for some fresh air.

Pip soon felt a bit better.

When they came back in,
the tree looked rather bare.

"Shall we make some paper
decorations now?" said Pip.

"That's a VERY good idea, Pip,"
said Posy.

So they made paperchains,
and stars and hearts.

And the tree looked beautiful.

Early next morning, Pip and Posy found **presents** under the Christmas tree.

They decided to open the little ones first.

Posy's present was a nice, new pair
of spotty scissors. And Pip's was . . .

a lovely rainbow
toothbrush!

"That's **just** what I need," said Pip.
Hooray!

Happy Christmas,
Pip and Posy!